This book belongs to

_____

We would like to extend a special thank
you to our parents. Leonard & Cecile,
Richard & Mary June for creating many
great Christmas traditions throughout
our childhoods. The yearly stroll around
the Christmas tree farms looking for that
perfect tree, will never be forgotten.

Thank you to all of our readers. Have fun
creating your own Christmas memories
and traditions with Glee.

Published by:
Indigo Beach House
Coral, PA 15731
www.indigobeachhouse.com

Written by David and Catherine King
www.santasglee.com

Illustrated by Toby Mikle
www.tmcreations.com

Edited by Dr. Kenneth Sherwood
*We would like to extend a special thank you to Dr. Sherwood
for taking the time to edit this book.*

Printed by Crown Media & Printing, Inc.
PO Box 606
Liberty Lake, WA 99019
www.crownmediacorp.com

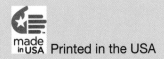

Santa's Glee

by David and
Catherine King

Indiana, Pa
4020 MILES

You've heard of all the reindeer
who live with Santa and his sleigh.

Christmas Tree
Capital of the
World

Now here's the story of
Glee who lives in Indiana, PA.

Indiana, Pennsylvania is famous for its Christmas trees.

Drive through the scenic hillsides
and they're so easy to see.

Glee is Santa's white reindeer
with a job that is hard to do.

He takes care of the world's
Christmas trees until they
come home to you.

He can move from place to place
at a speed that's faster than light.

From field to field and then back
again to ensure the trees grow right.

So what would Christmas be like without the Christmas tree?

Every size, shape, and color,
they all rely on Glee.

As the Christmas season grows near,
Glee's duties for Christmas extend.

He visits the homes of boys and girls
until the season ends.

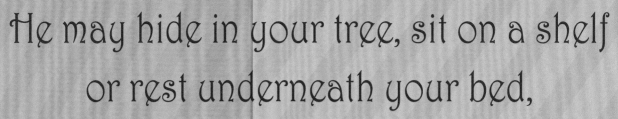

He may hide in your tree, sit on a shelf or rest underneath your bed,

all the time taking careful notes
on every word that is said.

Then off to the North Pole
Glee flies with great speed

with a note for Santa and his elves
that they will most certainly read.

will get all good reports
and a Merry Christmas too!

Kids who use poor manners
and have not learned to be good

will disappoint Glee and Santa
and not have the Christmas they could.

Now as our story continues
we'll look at two sisters quite small,

and how they act at Christmas
and what they can teach us all.

Ava and Julia are good little girls
whose ages are four and six.

They're writing their lists to Santa
with all their Christmas picks.

Shiny new bikes, a winter coat
and a new board game,

a new swimsuit and goggles
are a few of the things they name.

Now that their letters to Santa
have been written with thought and care

they must always work together,
keep things clean, and remember to share.

One day right before Christmas
the girls start to yell and fight.

They did not listen to what they were told
and aren't having a very good night.

Glee gives a note to Santa
with all the things that were bad.
As Santa reads the note aloud
he cannot help but be sad.

Julia and Ava are back at their house
looking around for Glee.

Because of their poor behavior,
he is nowhere that they can see.

Although they miss Glee,
they understand why
Glee cannot be found.

They must act nice
like they've been taught
for Glee to come back around.

Julia and Ava have learned a lesson
and begin to follow the rules.

They brush their teeth, clean their rooms
and behave at home and school.

Glee's next report to Santa
makes him smile from ear to ear.

The good news that Glee brings him
is just what he wanted to hear.

Glee goes back to the girls
to prepare for Christmas Day.

They have a lot of work to do
but first it's time to play.

Julia, Ava, and Glee
spend their time on Christmas Eve,

making cookies and peeling carrots
for Santa and reindeer to receive.

Christmas morning comes at last
and there are presents under the tree.

Santa has been to their house
but the girls cannot find Glee.

They find a note from Glee

I really enjoyed being here! I must return to the Christmas trees. I'll see you again next year.

Glee

Add your favorite pictures of us throughout these pages